JEREMY VISICK

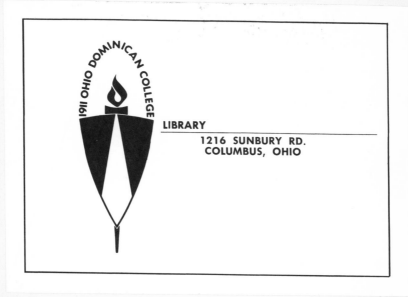

J
W

Library of Congress Cataloging-in-Publication Data

Wiseman, David.
  Jeremy Visick.
  Summary: Twelve-year-old Matthew is drawn almost against his will to help a boy his own age who was lost in a mining disaster a century before.
  ISBN 0-395-30449-0
  [1. Space and time—Fiction. 2. Miners—Fiction. 3. Cornwall, Eng.—Fiction]
I. Title.
PZ7.W78024Je   80-28116
[Fic]

Printed in the United States of America

RNF ISBN 0-395-30449-0
PAP ISBN 0-395-56153-1

AGM 10 9 8 7 6 5 4 3 2 1